W9-BHE-835

Here's what kids and grown-ups have to say about the Magic Tree House® books:

"Oh, man . . . the Magic Tree House series is really exciting!"
—Christina

"I like the Magic Tree House series. I stay up all night reading them. Even on school nights!"
—Peter

"Jack and Annie have opened a door to a world of literacy that I know will continue throughout the lives of my students."
—Deborah H.

"As a librarian, I have seen many happy young readers coming into the library to check out the next Magic Tree House book in the series."
—Lynne H.

Magic Tree House®

For a list of Magic Tree House® Merlin Missions and other Magic Tree House® titles, visit MagicTreeHouse.com.

MAGIC TREE HOUSE®

#35 CAMP TIME IN CALIFORNIA

BY MARY POPE OSBORNE

ILLUSTRATIONS BY AG FORD

A STEPPING STONE BOOK™

Random House 🏠 New York

For Michael Lipson

Text copyright © 2021 by Mary Pope Osborne
Cover art and interior illustrations copyright © 2021 by AG Ford

Visit us on the Web!
rhcbooks.com
MagicTreeHouse.com

Educators and librarians, for a variety of teaching tools, visit us at
RHTeachersLibrarians.com

Library of Congress Cataloging-in-Publication Data
Names: Osborne, Mary Pope, author. | Ford, AG, illustrator.
Title: Camp time in California / by Mary Pope Osborne; illustrated by AG Ford.
Description: New York: Random House Children's Books, [2021] | Series: Magic tree house; #35 | "A Stepping Stone Book." | Summary: "When the magic tree house whisks Jack and Annie back in time, they land in the tallest tree in Yosemite, California, where they join nature conservationist John Muir and US President Teddy Roosevelt on a historic trip through the woods" —Provided by publisher.
Identifiers: LCCN 2020031804 (print) | LCCN 2020031805 (ebook) | ISBN 978-0-593-17746-4 (hardcover) | ISBN 978-0-593-17747-1 (library binding) ISBN 978-0-593-17748-8 (ebook) | ISBN 978-0-593-17749-5 (paperback)
Subjects: CYAC: Time travel—Fiction. | Nature—Fiction. | Muir, John, 1838–1914—Fiction. | Roosevelt, Theodore, 1858–1919—Fiction. | Magic—Fiction. | Tree houses—Fiction. | Yosemite National Park (Calif.)—Fiction. | California—History—19th century—Fiction.
Classification: LCC PZ7.O81167 Cam 2021 (print) | LCC PZ7.O81167 (ebook) | DDC [Fic]—dc23

Printed in the United States of America

10 9 8 7 6 5 4 3 2 1

This book has been officially leveled by using the F&P Text Level Gradient™ Leveling System.

CONTENTS

PROLOGUE

One summer day in Frog Creek, Pennsylvania, a mysterious tree house appeared in the woods. It was filled with books. A boy named Jack and his sister, Annie, found the tree house and soon discovered that it was magic. They could go to any time and place in history just by pointing to a picture in one of the books. While they were gone, no time at all passed back in Frog Creek.

Jack and Annie eventually found out that the tree house belonged to Morgan le Fay, a magical librarian from the legendary realm of Camelot.

Since then, they have traveled on many adventures in the magic tree house and completed many missions for Morgan.

On their last several adventures, Jack and Annie learned great wisdom from heroes of the past.

Morgan is now sending them on another quest. On these journeys, they must help different creatures in the wondrous world of nature.

1

CALIFORNIA!

One summer evening after dinner, Jack sat in the living room. He was reading a book.

"What are you doing?" said Annie, coming down the stairs.

"Reading about llamas and the Andes Mountains," Jack said.

"Learning good stuff?" asked Annie.

"Good and bad," said Jack. "Logging is destroying a lot of the mountain forests."

"What does *logging* mean?" asked Annie.

"Cutting down trees for lumber," said Jack.

"In some places, it's against the law. It can be a disaster for wildlife." An evening breeze gusted into the house. "Could you close the front door, please?"

"Sure." Annie crossed to the door. Instead of closing it, she gazed out at the twilight.

"Close it, please?" said Jack.

"Whoa!" said Annie.

"Whoa what?" said Jack, looking up.

Annie turned to Jack. "The tree house is calling. It said, *'Come to me! Come!'*"

"You're making that up," said Jack.

"Sort of. It didn't say words. I *feel* it's out there," said Annie.

"Really?" said Jack. Annie's feelings about the tree house were always right.

"Let's go check," said Annie. "Ten minutes."

"Fourteen," said Jack, standing up. "It takes seven minutes to go there and seven minutes to come back."

4

"Got it!" said Annie. She called out, "Mom! Dad! Can Jack and I go out for fourteen minutes? Before it's totally dark?"

"Fourteen, no more!" their dad called back.

"Come on!" Jack said to Annie.

He and Annie pulled on hoodies and slipped out the front door. They ran across their yard.

"Wait, wait!" said Jack, stopping. "I forgot my backpack—"

"Leave it," said Annie, pulling him along. "We only have fourteen minutes."

Jack sighed and kept going. In the last light of day, he and Annie ran up the sidewalk. The first star of the night shone in the sky. A few cars passed them. Dogs barked from their yards.

Soon Jack and Annie came to the Frog Creek woods. They hurried between the quiet, familiar trees to the tallest oak.

Jack saw the tree house against the dusky sky.

"Good work!" he said to Annie. Then he grabbed the rope ladder and started up. Annie followed.

Jack and Annie climbed inside the tree house and looked around. In the fading light, they saw two books on the floor. Beside each book was a pencil.

"*Two* books?" said Jack. Morgan always gave them only one book to guide them on their journeys.

Jack and Annie each picked up a book. They read a single word on both covers:

YOSEMITE

"Yoze-might?" said Annie.

Jack laughed. "No, it's pronounced yo-SEH-mih-tee," he said. "Yosemite."

"What is that?" asked Annie.

"I've heard of it," said Jack. "I'm pretty sure it's some special nature place in California."

"California? Wow, I'd love to go back to California," said Annie.

7

"Me too," said Jack.

He opened his book. The first page was blank. The second and third pages were blank, too. He flipped through all the pages. "What's going on?" he said. "My whole book is blank."

"Mine too," said Annie. As she held up her book, a slip of paper fell out. "Oh! A note from Morgan!" Annie unfolded the note and read aloud:

The trees are calling.
Hurry and go
Into the forest,
Through sunshine and snow.

Call yourselves artists.
Draw what you see.
Give help to others.
Give it for free.

Before you go home,
Speak truth to power.
Help save the wilderness
By Sunday's noon hour.

Annie looked at Jack. "Sounds fun!" she said. "Let's go!"

"Wait, read the last lines again," said Jack.

Annie read:

Help save the wilderness
By Sunday's noon hour.

"So, what does that mean?" said Jack. "'Save the wilderness'? How's that even possible?"

9

Annie frowned. "Hmm. Let's ask that question later, when we know more," she said. "I can't wait to make a book with drawings! *That* sounds fun, doesn't it?"

"Sort of . . . I really can't draw," said Jack.

"I'm not great at drawing, either," said Annie, "but I still love doing it."

"Okay, let's go," said Jack. He was eager to see a different part of California. They hadn't been there since the San Francisco earthquake of 1906. "I'll point to *YOSEMITE* and see if that works."

Jack pointed to the word on the cover of his blank book. "I wish we could go there!" he said.

"California, here we come!" said Annie.

The wind started to blow.

The tree house started to spin.

It spun faster and faster.

Then everything was still.

Absolutely still.

2

LAND OF GIANTS

Yosemite was cool and very dark.

"Mmm. Smells good," said Annie.

Jack inhaled the woodsy smell of damp earth, green leaves, and tree bark.

"It's too dark to see anything, but I can tell my clothes magically changed," said Annie.

Jack felt his clothes. "Mine too," he said. "Feels like I'm wearing a heavy jacket, long pants, and"—he reached down to his feet—"leather boots?"

"I think I'm wearing the same thing!" said Annie. "And my jacket has huge pockets. They're so big I can put my sketchbook and pencil inside."

"Great, me too," said Jack. He dropped his book and pencil into one of his jacket pockets. He put Morgan's message in the other.

"Where are we?" said Annie. "Can we see anything?"

Jack and Annie looked out the window. The branches above the tree house were dense with dark leaves. But between leaves and branches, Jack could see pale gray sky.

"Is it dawn?" asked Annie.

"Or dusk?" said Jack.

"Hard to tell," said Annie. "We'll find out soon. Let's go down."

"Okay, but go slow," said Jack.

"You too," said Annie. She found the opening in the floor and started down the rope ladder.

Jack followed. A mild wind blew through the

tree limbs. The leaves made swishing, whispery sounds.

"Hold on!" Jack called.

"You too!" Annie called back.

In the dark, Jack tightly gripped the sides of the ladder. He moved his hands and feet slowly down . . . and down . . . step by step . . . step by step. . . .

The breeze grew stronger, then softer. The *swishing* sounds rose and fell.

"This ladder's incredibly long!" Annie yelled.

"Yeah, because this tree's incredibly tall!" said Jack.

"Don't be worried!" said Annie.

"I'm not worried," said Jack. Actually, he *was* worried. *No tree in the world could be as tall as this,* he thought. The sound of windblown leaves was starting to sound spooky.

The high, sweet twitter of a bird came from nearby. Then another. And another.

It was dawn! "Yay," Jack whispered.

"It's getting lighter!" said Annie. "And we're almost there!"

Jack looked down. *Yes!* The ground was only about twenty feet below!

Jack and Annie kept climbing down. Finally they reached the bottom of the tree and stepped off the ladder.

"Hey, we *are* dressed alike," said Annie.

"Yep," said Jack. In the dim, shadowy light, he could see that their clothes *had* magically changed into canvas jackets, heavy cloth pants, and leather boots with laces.

Jack looked up. He could see a bit of pink sky above the treetop.

"Oh, man," he said. "This must be the tallest tree in the world! It's like a twenty-story building! And check out the trunk!"

"It's beautiful!" said Annie. She took off running around the massive reddish-brown trunk.

"I'll bet thirty kids could stand around this tree!" she said when she got back to Jack.

"More like fifty!" said Jack. "And all the trees look as big as this one!"

In the cool morning air, every tree seemed as high as a twenty-story building.

"Did we come to a land of giants?" Annie asked breathlessly. "Or did we shrink?"

Jack laughed. "Just the trees are giants," he said. "The squirrels are normal size, see?" He pointed to a squirrel scampering over the forest floor.

"Oh, right," said Annie. She looked around. "Is *this* the wilderness we're supposed to save?"

"I don't think so . . . ," said Jack. The gigantic trees looked super healthy and strong.

"Maybe there's another wilderness nearby?" said Annie.

"That doesn't sound right, either," said Jack.

"Well, we can figure it out later," said Annie. "I can't wait to start drawing." She pulled out her pencil and sketchbook.

"Seriously, I really can't draw," said Jack.

"Just try," said Annie. "I'll sketch that butterfly." She pointed to a delicate white butterfly perched on a leaf. "You can draw the squirrel."

The little squirrel was now nibbling a tree cone.

"Nah, too ordinary," said Jack.

"Do it for practice," said Annie. She crept closer to the white butterfly.

Jack opened his book. He set the sharp point of his pencil on a blank page and stared at the squirrel.

Suddenly Jack's pencil seemed to take on a life of its own. Before Jack could think, he drew the squirrel's head. He drew its dark eyes and small ears.

"Whoa!" said Jack.

"Wow!" yelled Annie, drawing the butterfly. "Our pencils are magic!"

"Yes!" cried Jack. He swiftly sketched the squirrel's body. He drew its long rear legs and short front legs and tiny hands holding the tree cone. He shaded the squirrel's fur on its belly, back, and bushy tail.

Soon he was done.

Jack smiled at the real squirrel. He knew the little creature really well now. It didn't seem ordinary at all.

"Look!" said Annie, holding up her sketch. "Perfect butterfly!"

"Perfect squirrel!" said Jack, showing his drawing.

"WE'RE ARTISTS!" cried Annie.

3

GRIZZLY!

"I can't believe it," Jack said with a laugh. "This is so cool!"

"I know! I want to draw everything!" said Annie. "I'll sketch that little bird!" She pointed to a small red bird sitting on a low branch. Then she turned the page in her book and started sketching.

What next? Jack eagerly looked around. A large mushroom caught his attention. He lightly held his magic pencil and began sketching.

Jack outlined the graceful curves of the mushroom's cap and stem. Then his pencil moved up and down, drawing the hundreds of fanlike folds under the cap.

Soon Jack held up his work. "Perfect mushroom!" he exclaimed.

"Perfect bird!" said Annie. "Oh, shh! There's a deer."

Not far away, a deer with antlers was eating the leaves of a bush. "I'll draw him!" Annie whispered, and tiptoed through the forest.

Jack gazed around at the giant trees.

He began outlining a huge trunk. He drew the deep grooves in the rusty-red bark. He shaded the furrows.

As Jack sketched the tree trunk, a gust of wind made the high branches sway. Jack looked up. Millions of leaves seemed to be waving at him.

Jack stared in awe. "Hi, there," he said to the tree. Then he grinned. Was he really talking to a tree now? He shook his head and looked around for Annie.

21

Where was she? Annie and the deer were gone.

Jack started through the forest. "Annie!" he called. He walked around one giant trunk, then another, until he saw Annie. She was standing in a ray of misty light slanting between the trees.

"Hey!" said Jack.

Annie turned and held her finger to her lips.

Jack stepped softly toward her. Annie pointed to a hollow in one of the giant trunks.

"Whoa!" said Jack, stepping back.

A huge bear was asleep inside. The bear had shaggy brown fur and long sharp claws.

"Sweet, huh?" Annie whispered.

"*Not* sweet," Jack whispered back. "That's a *grizzly* bear."

"Oh. Okay. But it's fast asleep," whispered Annie. "I want to draw it."

"Are you nuts?" said Jack. "Grizzly bears attack humans. Their jaws are so strong, they can bite through a bowling ball."

"No way," said Annie.

"I read that!" Jack exclaimed.

The grizzly stirred and opened its eyes. It looked at Jack and Annie.

"Yikes," said Annie.

The grizzly bear huffed and hauled itself out of the hollow in the trunk. Standing on its hind legs, it looked like it was at least eight feet tall.

"And I—I read that if you run into a bear, you

should stay calm," Jack whispered. "Act friendly. Wave your arms."

Annie waved both her arms. "Howdy," she said.

Oh, brother, thought Jack.

The bear stood still and stared at them.

"How are you doing?" Annie asked brightly.

The bear went back down on all fours. Its head was lowered, its ears back. Then it roared.

"Bad sign," said Jack. He clutched Annie's arm. He pulled her farther away from the bear.

"Should we run?" she asked.

"No. Bears run as fast as horses," said Jack.

The bear growled a deep, low growl.

"Run!" said Jack.

He and Annie took off through the green-and-brown forest. They tore around the enormous

tree trunks. They scrambled over chunks of bark, fallen leaves, tree cones, seedlings, plants, logs, and rocks. They ran until they came to a dirt trail.

"Wait . . . wait," said Annie, huffing and puffing. She grabbed Jack and stopped him. "Is it still coming?"

They both panted as they looked behind them.

There was no sign of the grizzly.

"Where is it?" said Jack.

"Maybe it didn't chase us," said Annie.

"Or maybe it's hiding," said Jack.

"Listen, I hear something," said Annie.

Jack heard heavy thumping against the ground.

"Come on!" he said.

"No, no, wait!" said Annie. "That sounds like horses!"

A moment later, four men on horseback rounded a bend in the forest trail. The horsemen rode in a line toward Jack and Annie.

The first rider was an odd-looking cowboy. He

wore a cowboy hat and a bandanna. His baggy pants were tucked into tall riding boots. He had a thick mustache and wore round glasses.

The second rider was tall and thin. He had a scraggly white beard and wore a shabby overcoat and hat.

The last two men wore blue overalls. Behind them were two pack mules without riders.

As the group drew close to Jack and Annie, the cowboy held up his hand. The horsemen and mules behind him came to a noisy halt.

"Greetings, friends!" the cowboy shouted.

4

BULLY FOR YOU!

"Greetings!" Annie said.

"Did a newspaper send you kids to spy on us?" the cowboy asked with a grin.

What's he talking about? Jack wondered.

"No, sir!" said Annie. "My brother and I were running from a bear."

"A grizzly bear," added Jack.

"Oh, I'm sorry, but you can't fool us, sonny," the cowboy said. "No grizzlies in Yosemite now. The last one was spotted eight years ago. Right, John?" He looked at the older, bearded man.

"That's right, sir," said John. His blue eyes twinkled as he smiled at Jack and Annie. "You must have seen a black bear. They won't hurt you if you leave them alone. They mostly eat plants, roots, and berries."

"But it looked just like a grizzly," said Jack. "It had shaggy brown fur and really long claws."

"Sorry, son," said the cowboy. "You have to trust my friend—we all call him John of the Mountains. He knows this wild country better than anybody. For thirty years he's been studying the animals, trees, and rocks of Yosemite."

"Cool," said Annie. "We're studying all that, too, and drawing pictures of it."

"Good for you, young lady," said the cowboy. "Well, we must be on our way. If you're afraid of bears, take my advice: Walk softly and carry a big stick!" The cowboy laughed heartily at his own joke. The other riders laughed, too.

"Wait, would you like to see our drawings?" said Annie.

"Uh . . . no, Annie," said Jack. He could tell the riders wanted to get going.

But Annie pulled out her sketchbook. She held it up to the cowboy. "Check it out!" she said.

The cowboy took the book from Annie. He opened it and looked at her butterfly drawing. "*You* drew this?" he said.

"Yes. Yes, sir," said Annie. "We're artists."

"Well, bully for you!" said the cowboy.

"Wait till you see my brother's drawings," said Annie. "Show him, Jack."

Jack shyly handed his sketchbook to the cowboy.

"Excellent . . . ," the man said, staring at Jack's squirrel drawing. "Here, John—take a look." The cowboy handed both books to John of the Mountains.

The elderly man looked at the butterfly and squirrel sketches. His face broke into a wide grin. "Goodness! You two are serious artists," he said. "What are your names?"

"Jack and Annie," said Annie.

"Well, Jack and Annie, you perfectly captured the rare Alpine butterfly and the Douglas squirrel," John said. "Did you know that the Douglas squirrel is the spirit of the sequoia trees? When he eats a cone from a big tree, he scatters its seeds. From those tiny seeds, a few trees might sprout. Over hundreds of years, they'll grow into the mighty giants of Yosemite."

"Wow," said Annie. "That shows how everything is connected, doesn't it?"

John of the Mountains looked startled. "Yes, it does, Annie," he said. "One little thing in nature— like that squirrel—is hitched to the whole universe."

"Exactly!" said Jack, trying to join the conversation.

John shook his head in wonder. "You two are remarkable," he said. "How did you get here? Who brought you?"

"Um . . . our art teacher delivered us," said Jack.

"Her name is Morgan," said Annie. "She dropped us off near the big trees."

"Hold on," the cowboy growled. "Are you saying your teacher just left you alone in the woods?"

"Uh . . . well . . . ," stammered Jack. He looked at Annie.

"It's okay. We asked her to leave us in the wilderness overnight," said Annie. "We told her we wanted to spend time in Yosemite to make our nature books. She thought it would be a great opportunity for us."

"I don't agree," said the cowboy, scowling. "It's quite risky to leave two children in the wild."

"Sometimes it might be," said Annie. "But not for Jack and me. We're actually tougher than we look. And smarter. And braver."

John of the Mountains laughed. "I believe you, Annie," he said. He turned to the cowboy. "Sir, did you not say you wished that nature artists could travel with us?"

"I did," said the cowboy.

"Well, two excellent young artists have just crossed our path," said John of the Mountains. "And they plan to spend a night in Yosemite. I call that a miracle."

"I still think they're too young," said the cowboy.

"Sir, I was out in the world, working for my family, when I was their age," said John. "Won't they be safer with us on our journey than wandering the woods alone?"

Wait. Journey? Where are they going? Jack wondered.

The cowboy looked at Jack and Annie.

Annie stood straighter and held her chin up.

"All right, you win, John," the cowboy said, chuckling. "Would you two young artists like to join us?"

"Yes! We would!" said Annie.

We would? thought Jack. He wasn't sure.

"We will pay you for your work," the cowboy said.

Annie whispered Morgan's words to Jack, *"Give help to others. Give it for free."*

"Um . . . no thank you, sir. We only work for free," said Jack. "But can you tell us where we're going?"

"Of course!" the cowboy said with a toothy grin. "We're going *nowhere*, son! We're planning to get lost in the wild!"

5

LOST IN THE WILD

Lost in the wild? thought Jack.

"All right, Jack and Annie!" said John of the Mountains. "Our forest rangers will prepare the pack mules for you."

"Thanks!" said Annie. "That sounds like fun."

"Charlie!" John called to one of the men in blue overalls. "You and Archie make room on our pack mules for our nature artists!"

"Yes, sir!" said Charlie.

The gray mules were smaller than the horses. They had long ears, thick heads, and skinny legs.

Both had pack saddles with bulky, side bundles. The rangers shifted the cargo forward to make room for Jack and Annie.

"Climb on, partners!" said Charlie.

With the rangers' help, Jack and Annie mounted the two mules. They sat on the back of the saddles with the bundles pushed to the front. They clutched the straps that held everything together.

"Be careful. A mule will always try to make a fool of you!" said Charlie. Then he walked off.

"Not this one," said Annie. "I love your bunny ears," she said to her mule. "I'll call you Petey, for Peter Rabbit." She turned to Jack. "You could name yours Benny, for Benjamin Bunny."

"Not. Going. To. Happen," Jack said dryly.

"All set?" the cowboy boomed from the front of the line. "On through the wild! Remember—our aim is to steer clear of all civilization!"

As Jack's mule plodded at the end of the line, Jack bumped up and down. With no way to guide his mule, he felt out of control.

The group left the dirt trail. Soon they were slowly climbing up a rocky path.

"Hey, John of the Mountains!" Annie called out to John, who was riding in front of her. "What's the name of the cowboy with the mustache?"

John looked over his shoulder. "You don't recognize him?" he asked.

"Nope," said Annie.

John smiled. "His name is Teddy," he said.

"Oh, wow," said Annie. "We once had a great friend named Teddy. He was a dog."

John laughed. "Good. Think of *this* Teddy as a friend, too," he said. "But call him Sir."

"*Sir?* Okay. But what does Sir do?" asked Annie.

"Many things," said John. "Years ago, he was commander of the Rough Riders in the Spanish-American War."

"Who are the Rough Riders?" Jack called.

"You might call them volunteer cowboy soldiers," said John.

"Cool," said Annie.

"Whoa," Jack said to his mule. At the moment, he was having a rough ride himself. His mule was skittish. It kept veering to the right or the left.

Soon Jack and the mule were trailing far behind. Jack was embarrassed that he couldn't keep up with Annie and the others.

Suddenly a rabbit dashed across the trail. Jack's mule lurched off the rocky path. Jack let go of the strap. He lost his balance and fell to the ground.

Annie turned to look. "Stop, everyone!" she shouted. "Jack fell off his mule!"

All the riders came to a halt. Teddy rode back to Jack.

While his mule munched on a shrub, Jack stood up and brushed himself off. He felt his face turn red. He wanted to disappear.

"Are you all right?" Teddy boomed. "Did he throw you?"

"No, sir. It was my fault," said Jack. "I made a mistake, and I lost my balance."

"Aw, don't worry about it, son," said Teddy. "The person who never makes a mistake is the one who never tries anything."

"Yes, sir," said Jack.

"Be positive, Jack," said Teddy. "Talk to

yourself. Say *'I can ride this mule!'* If you believe that, you're halfway there." Teddy flashed a grin. "I personally know that you can succeed at this, Jack." The cowboy tipped his hat. Then he rode back to the head of the line.

Jack took a deep breath. He wanted to measure up to Teddy's belief in him. "I can do this," he mumbled to himself. "I can totally ride a mule."

Jack climbed back onto his mule. He talked in a whisper to himself. "I can ride a mule. I can do this. I can keep up. I can do this. . . ."

The mule seemed to hear Jack's words. Soon it was keeping a steady pace behind the others.

Teddy looked back and waved his hat at Jack. "Good work, Jack!" he called.

Jack waved and smiled. As he bumped along on his mule, he no longer felt worried. Forgetting himself, he looked eagerly at the passing scenery— shrubs, birds, wildflowers. He wanted to stop and sketch everything.

After a while, Teddy held up his hand and brought the group to a halt. Jack and Annie hopped down from their mules. The others dismounted from their horses.

Teddy was not nearly as tall as he seemed on horseback, Jack realized. But the stout, cheerful cowboy still seemed larger than life.

"Chow time!" Teddy bellowed.

6

ROUGH RIDERS

The two rangers opened the saddlebags. They handed out pieces of cold chicken, chunks of dry bread, and canteens.

After a quick bite of bread and a drink of water, Jack pulled out his sketchbook. Annie did the same. With their magic pencils, they started sketching.

Annie sketched a cedar tree, and Jack drew a pile of boulders shining in the noon sun. He quickly sketched lines and curves, adding shadow and light.

While Jack and Annie sketched, John studied a stone with a magnifying glass. Teddy imitated bird calls.

Teddy made a quick zipping sound: *fitz-bew! fitz-bew!*

"Willow flycatcher!" said John, without looking up from the stone he was studying.

Teddy made high, short whistle sounds.

"Lark sparrow!" said John, still peering through his magnifying glass. Jack could tell that Teddy and John had played this game before.

Teddy twittered: *kew-kew-kew.*

"Dark-eyed Junco," Annie said.

John looked up. He and Teddy laughed. "Wonderful, Annie!" said John.

Jack laughed, too. He was proud of Annie. But he wished he also knew bird calls. Annie had learned them from Uncle Josh.

Teddy clapped his hands together. "It's time to

be on our way!" he said. "Let's get further lost in the wild!"

Jack and Annie put away their sketchbooks. They walked back to their mules and climbed on.

Riding along the trail, Jack looked around. Again, he wanted to draw everything he saw: tree stumps, weeds, wildflowers, birds.

As the horses and mules climbed higher, clouds covered the sun. The air turned colder.

To Jack's surprise, snowflakes began falling. The wind began to blow. Soon the whole sky was dark gray.

"Oh, man," whispered Jack. His teeth chattered.

The wind from the sudden snowstorm blew harder, until Jack could hardly see. He shivered and wished they could find shelter.

The riders kept going. Their mules and horses plodded up a snow-covered trail. Jack's face was freezing in the blinding white mist.

"I love wild weather!" Teddy shouted.

"I agree! There's nothing more fun!" shouted John of the Mountains.

Are they joking? thought Jack. He couldn't feel his hands anymore. His fingers were as stiff and frozen as icicles.

"You kids okay back there?" Teddy called to Jack and Annie.

"Yes, sir! I love snow!" shouted Annie.

"Life's a grand adventure, isn't it?" called Teddy.

"Yes, sir!" Jack shouted. But to himself, he whispered, "This is the worst! We're freezing to death! We're lost! We're tired!"

Just before Jack lost all hope, the weather changed again.

The snow stopped falling.

The wind stopped blowing.

The sun broke through the clouds. The sky turned from gray to blue.

47

Jack heard laughter from John of the Mountains. "I promised you wild weather, sir!" he called to Teddy. "Did I not deliver?"

"Indeed you did, my friend! Thank you!" shouted Teddy. "Glacier Point soon! And camp time!"

After a short ride, the horses and mules came to a halt on a flat part of the trail. The ground ahead was bordered by pine trees.

Teddy and John jumped down from their horses. The two men climbed some boulders and disappeared over the top of a ledge.

Jack and Annie hopped off their mules.

Annie pulled out her sketchbook. "Let's draw!" she said to Jack.

"You go ahead. I need to rest a minute," he said.

Annie sat on a rock and began sketching the pine trees. Charlie gathered branches to make a fire. Archie tended to the animals.

Jack sat alone. He was sore from the mule ride.

His hands and face still hurt from the freezing snow. *Annie is always so strong and happy and confident,* he thought. Why wasn't he more like her? Why wasn't he more like Teddy and John and Charlie and Archie? What was wrong with him?

"Jack! Annie!" John called from above. "Come see the view from the overlook!"

Annie stopped sketching the pines and leaped to her feet. "Let's go!" Annie said.

"No, you go ahead. Look at the view without me," said Jack.

"Really? Oh, please come," Annie said. "I want you to see it, too."

Jack sighed. "Okay," he said. He dragged himself up from the ground and followed Annie. They scrambled over the boulders to the overlook.

"WOW!" said Annie.

Jack gasped. It was the greatest view he'd ever seen. A deep valley was bordered by rock formations as high as mountains. A roaring waterfall

plunged down a sheer rock wall. The massive rocks and water were shimmering in the golden light of the Yosemite sunset.

Teddy was gazing through binoculars at a vast open space.

"Winter snows are melting everywhere," said John. "Everything is alive! Waters flow! Fish swim! Birds fly!"

"Bully for spring!" said Teddy.

The others laughed. Jack laughed, too. He was so overwhelmed by the view, he forgot how tired and achy he felt. He forgot to worry about himself.

"This valley was formed millions of years ago by glaciers," said John. "And that's the tallest waterfall in the United States. In full moonlight, it's an incredible sight."

"I'd love to see that," said Jack.

"Perhaps someday you will," said John. "But tonight, we have only a slender new moon."

Slowly, the sun slipped behind the high rocks

and the waterfall. The sky changed from gold to purple.

Teddy put his binoculars away. He turned to Jack and Annie and smiled. "You were both true Rough Riders today," he said, "weathering the snowstorm on the back of your mules, never complaining, never stopping. Life is a grand adventure, is it not?"

"Yes, sir," said Annie.

"Yes, sir," said Jack. "It is."

And this time, he meant it.

7

EYES ON THE STARS

"Suppertime!" Charlie called from below.

"Wonderful! I'm starving!" Teddy exclaimed.

Teddy, John, Jack, and Annie climbed back down to the campsite.

The crisp mountain air smelled of woodsmoke.

Charlie and Archie were cooking over a campfire.

Everyone sat on logs close to the warm, crackling heat. Charlie passed out plates piled with fried chicken, steak, and bread.

Teddy spoke to John between big mouthfuls

of food. "So. Tell me everything you're worried about."

"Many things, sir," said John. "Hunters and trappers have overrun the valley. Black bears and wolverines are being caught and killed in steel traps."

"What?" said Annie.

"Shh," said Jack. He wanted to hear John and Teddy. Their conversation sounded important.

"What is the biggest threat to the wilderness? What do you fear most?" Teddy asked John.

"I fear greed, sir. Human greed," said John. "Some want to clear the land here and build hotels and shops. Some try to slaughter the most beautiful birds just to sell their feathers for hats!"

"That's terrible," Annie whispered to Jack.

"But I believe I may grieve most for the big trees, sir," said John. "Some companies want to cut down the mighty giants only to make money! They think the forests are merely factories for wood! Only a few years ago, one of the oldest trees in the grove was cut down."

"Oh, no!" Annie said to Jack.

"Thieves! Scoundrels!" said Teddy.

"Yes," said John. "That tree was one of the largest living things on this earth. Fourteen hundred years old. It took three weeks to saw down the mighty giant."

Annie softly moaned. She put her face in her hands.

"It's okay," Jack whispered to her, though he didn't think it was okay. How could anyone want to destroy one of the most incredible trees on earth?

Teddy heaved a sigh. "Well, you've given me much to think about, John," he said. He stood up and stretched. "It's time to say good night, friends. I love sleeping in the cool, clean mountain air. Keep your feet on the ground and your eyes on the stars."

Teddy headed to a stack of blankets prepared

by the rangers. He lay down on them, and within minutes, he was snoring loudly.

John turned his attention to Jack and Annie. "The rangers have prepared two nice piles of blankets for you over there," he said.

"Thank you," said Jack. Annie kept her head down.

"Is Annie okay?" John asked.

"I'm good, thanks," Annie said in a muffled voice.

"She's just tired," Jack said to John.

"So am I," said John kindly. "Well, get some rest. You both deserve it."

"Thank you," said Jack.

After John left, Jack gently patted Annie on the back. "Come on, let's go," he said.

Annie stumbled after him to their camp beds.

"A good night's sleep will make you feel better," said Jack, sounding like their mom.

Annie didn't say anything.

"Tomorrow will be a really fun day, I promise," said Jack.

"Thanks," Annie said in a small voice.

They both lay down. Exhausted and cold, Jack pulled his wool blankets tightly up to his chin. He was half asleep when something woke him. He looked around.

Annie was missing from her bed.

Jack jumped up. His heart was pounding.

Teddy was snoring louder than ever. John slept on the bare ground without blankets. The rangers slept near the fire.

Jack saw a small dark shape huddled near the animals. "Annie!" he whispered.

He hurried over and crouched down beside her. "Hey, what are you doing?"

"I just want to cry by myself," Annie said. "I—I can't stop thinking about that giant tree that was cut down. For over a thousand years, that tree held birds and squirrels. It raised its branches to the sky. It felt the wind and the sun and the rain. I wonder, did the tree feel anything when they were sawing it down? That's . . . that's what I keep wondering. . . ." She covered her face and shook with a sob.

"I don't know if trees feel," Jack said. He could hardly bear to think about it.

After a moment, he stood up. "Come on," he

said. "Let's do something. Let's climb up to the overlook. Maybe we can see the waterfall at night."

"I don't feel like it," said Annie.

Jack didn't feel like it, either, but he wanted to do something to help Annie. "It could be fun," he said.

"Okay." Annie wiped her face with her jacket sleeve and stood up. They walked to the dark boulders and started climbing.

Jack was the first to reach the top. "Whoa!" he said.

The dark purple sky was filled with countless dots of light.

"You're going to love this!" he whispered as Annie climbed over the ledge.

"Oh!" she breathed. "Billions of stars!"

"Incredible, huh?" said Jack.

"Yes," said Annie. "I don't get it—where have those stars been hiding all my life?"

"They're always there," said Jack. "Dad told

me city lights fill our night skies now. They drown out the light of distant stars. So, the best places to see stars are places like this, places without artificial light."

"I love those stars," said Annie.

"Me too," said Jack. "Hey, think about this: The stars will never go away. Even if the wilderness goes away, the stars won't."

Annie sighed. "Thanks. . . . You make me feel better," she said.

"Good," said Jack. But he knew she was saying that to make *him* feel better.

"Hey, let's try to draw them," said Jack.

"There's too many," said Annie.

"We can at least try," said Jack.

They both pulled out their sketchbooks. As they sat together on the ledge, Jack pressed his pencil against a blank white page.

Instead of drawing lines, his magic pencil started tapping the paper. Annie's did the same.

Their pencils tapped slowly at first . . . then faster and faster, until the tapping seemed lightning fast.

Even as Jack grew tired, his pencil kept tapping.

Even after Jack closed his eyes, his pencil kept tapping.

Even after Jack dozed off, his pencil kept tapping the page. . . .

8

NOONDAY SURPRISE

"Jack! Annie!" a voice called from the campsite.

"Jack, wake up," said Annie. "Charlie's calling us."

"Oh! What?" said Jack, opening his eyes.

"We're up here! We're coming!" Annie shouted back to Charlie.

Jack was still holding his pencil. "What happened?"

"We fell asleep drawing stars," said Annie.

Overhead, all the stars had vanished from sight.

In the pale dawn, Jack could see the valley below. He saw the huge rock formations and the high white waterfall.

He held up his sketchbook. He looked at his last sketch. "Oh, man, I don't believe this," he said.

"Look!" said Annie, holding up her book.

Both their drawings showed countless tiny silver dots on a black background. Their magic pencils had miraculously captured the full starry night sky over Yosemite.

"It looks just like what we saw," said Annie.

"Totally!" said Jack.

Birds started singing.

"It's a new morning," said Annie. She smiled. "Maybe it *will* be a fun day."

Jack was relieved. Annie seemed like her regular self.

"Jack! Annie!" Charlie shouted again.

"Coming!" Jack and Annie put their pencils

and sketchbooks back in their pockets. They scrambled down from the ledge.

Sunlight was shining on the campsite. John and Teddy were eating breakfast. Archie was packing up all the gear. Charlie held a skillet over a low fire.

"Come get your pancakes!" he called to Jack and Annie.

"Oh, boy!" said Jack. Sleeping in the open air had given him a big appetite.

"Good morning, friends!" said Teddy. "Up early sketching the view?"

"Up *late*," said Annie. "We sketched a billion stars."

Teddy laughed. "I hope you got 'em all," he said.

"Actually, we did," said Annie.

"May we see your sketches?" said John.

"Yes!" said Annie. She and Jack pulled out their sketchbooks and handed them to John and Teddy.

Jack and Annie ate their pancakes while the

two men looked carefully at their nature drawings—the squirrel, red bird, mushroom, tree trunk, butterfly, deer, boulders, cedar, pines, waterfall, rock formations, and starry night sky.

"Goodness, your work is remarkable," said John. "Your drawings capture both the majesty of Yosemite and the beauty of its small, everyday wonders."

"Thanks," said Jack and Annie.

At first, Teddy didn't speak. As he studied the sketchbooks, he kept shaking his head. Finally he looked up. "Words cannot express the full truth of nature's magic," he said. "But your drawings have done just that."

"Thank you, sir. We only wish we could save it," Annie said.

"Save what?" said Teddy.

"The wilderness," said Annie. "We wish no one would ever slaughter birds or catch animals in steel traps or cut down the giant trees."

66

"Really?" said Teddy. "Even as a child, you think about these things?"

"I *cry* about these things," said Annie.

"She does," said Jack.

Teddy stared thoughtfully at them.

"Ready to go, sir?" Charlie asked. "We need to be there by noon." The two forest rangers had packed up everything and saddled the horses and mules.

Teddy took a deep breath and let it out. "Yes, I believe I am," he said, standing. "Let us go now, my friends, and face civilization."

The four men mounted their horses. Jack and Annie climbed onto their mules. With Teddy in the lead, they all rode away from the campsite.

Soon Jack noticed something strange. Women and children were peeking out from behind trees along the trail.

"Who are *they*?" he asked Annie.

"I don't know," Annie said. "Look, there's

more." She pointed to a group farther along the trail.

As the riders drew closer to the crowd, everyone smiled and waved. Children jumped up and down with excitement.

Charlie rode to the front, shouting, "Step back! Please, step back!" He cleared the way, making a path for Teddy and the other riders.

The horses and mules quickened their pace and trotted past the onlookers.

"What's going on?" said Jack, looking over his shoulder. People were still waving at them.

"I don't know. But look—there's lots more," said Annie.

Up ahead, the trail widened. Jack could see hundreds of people standing outside a white, wooden hotel. Horse-drawn carriages were parked under trees.

As the riders drew closer, photographers

rushed forward and snapped photos of Teddy and John. The people in the crowd began cheering. Jack heard someone shout, "Mr. President! Mr. President!"

Mr. President? thought Jack. *Who's that?*

Teddy and John climbed off their horses. They shook hands with men in suits. A tall man led Teddy to the front steps of the hotel. The crowd pressed forward to hear him speak.

Jack and Annie sat on their mules and stared in shock.

"Is Teddy president of something?" asked Annie.

"Seems like it," said Jack.

"President of *what*?" said Annie.

"Ladies and gentlemen!" a tall man shouted. "Please welcome the president of the United States, Theodore Roosevelt!"

"Wha-at?" Jack nearly fell off his mule.

"Wow! Oh, wow!" cried Annie. As the crowd cheered wildly, she cheered, too. "Yay! Yay!"

Jack was too stunned to clap or cheer. He couldn't believe it. Teddy wasn't just a friendly, fearless cowboy.

Teddy was the president of the United States!

9

THE LAST GRIZZLY

"Thank you, Governor!" said President Teddy Roosevelt. "Ladies and gentlemen, I come to you having survived the backwoods! I have seen the true beauty of Yosemite! And I have had a bully good time!"

The crowd laughed and cheered.

"I must thank world-famous naturalist and writer, Mr. John Muir, or John of the Mountains as many of us call him, for guiding me," said President Roosevelt. "And I thank two young artists, Jack and Annie! I promise I will save this wilderness

for them! And for their children and for their children's children! And for all the people of this great nation, rich and poor!"

The crowd cheered.

"We must always preserve the birds and animals here, and, of course, the lives of our priceless giant trees!" said Teddy. "We are not building this beautiful country for a day. We want America to last through the ages! And so today I announce that, as president of these great United States, I am placing *all* of Yosemite under National Park protection!"

The crowd roared.

"Thank you for coming!" the president said. "Enjoy your Sunday!" Then, as the crowd kept cheering, the governor led Teddy into the hotel.

Annie looked at Jack. Her face was shining.

"We did it," Jack said. "We helped save the wilderness."

Annie nodded. *"By Sunday's noon hour,"* she said with a smile.

"Jack! Annie!" someone called.

They looked behind them.

John of the Mountains was on his horse again. He rode over to them.

"I want to thank you," he said. "My job was to guide President Roosevelt through Yosemite and convince him to put *all* of it—especially the big trees—under the protection of the National Park System. You helped me very much, and I'm grateful."

"You're welcome!" said Annie.

"Will you join me in the hotel for lunch?" John asked.

"Thanks, but we need to meet our art teacher now," said Annie. "We have to go back to the big trees where she left us."

"She's picking us up there," said Jack.

"I'm afraid the big trees are quite far from

74

here," said John. "But while the president meets with the governor, I can lead you there, then return with the mules."

"Uh . . . don't you want to go inside the hotel with the others?" said Annie.

"No. Actually, I always prefer to be outside rather than inside," said John. "Wait, I'll tell Charlie."

As John told the ranger his plans, Jack turned to Annie. "How will we climb up to the tree house if John's with us?"

She shrugged. "I guess we'll just hang out with him till he leaves," she said.

John rode back to them. Jack and Annie followed him on their mules. The three animals trotted away from the hotel grounds and started along the forest trail.

John led the way over the long, bumpy, winding road. On their journey, they again rode through different kinds of weather.

At first the day was hot and sunny, but then clouds moved in. The wind blew, the air grew colder. A hard rain fell.

Jack remembered Teddy's words. "I love wild weather!" he shouted. Annie laughed.

Suddenly the rain stopped, and warm sunlight returned.

By the time they reached the grove of big trees, it was nearly twilight.

Long shadows crossed the forest.

"Here we are!" said John.

Not far away was the giant tree with the magic tree house high in its branches. Fortunately, the rope ladder was out of sight on the other side of its massive trunk.

John got off his horse, and Jack and Annie jumped off their mules.

Annie hugged hers. "Thanks, Petey," she whispered.

"Good mule," Jack said to his. "Thanks for

taking me everywhere." The animal flicked its long ears and snorted.

As Jack walked away, Annie was still whispering to Petey. The mule seemed to be listening carefully to her.

John looked puzzled.

"Annie has a special way with animals," Jack explained. "She talks to them and listens to them and understands what they're feeling."

"Wonderful," said John. "Any glimpse into the hidden life of an animal makes our own lives better in every way."

"That's true," said Jack. He loved how John talked about nature.

"Is your teacher coming in a buggy?" John asked.

"Uh . . . yes," said Jack. "But you don't have to wait with us. You probably need to be somewhere else."

John shook his head. "For me, the best place to be is wherever I am."

Good attitude, thought Jack, *but not good for us when we need to climb into the tree house.*

"While we wait, I'll make a little fire to warm us up," said John. He quickly gathered kindling and branches, then lit a match.

Soon Jack and Annie were sitting close to a crackling fire. John took a small bundle from one of the saddlebags. "A bite to eat before your journey home," he said. He handed them chunks of hard bread.

As Jack crunched his snack, a breeze blew through the forest. The wind picked up. All the tall trees waved. Their leaves made swishing, whispery sounds.

"I love these giant sequoia trees as much as I love people," said John. "Every leaf on every tree seems to sing. Can you hear them?"

"Almost . . . ," whispered Annie.

Jack only heard the swishing sounds. He didn't hear singing.

"There's music in everything," said John, "falling water, stones, stars. Human senses are not fine enough to hear nature's song."

"I wish I could hear it," said Annie.

"You will," said John. "Just keep listening."

79

Jack looked around at the darkening forest, at the other giant trees, their leaves shaking in the wind.

Suddenly he nearly jumped out of his skin.

"Grizzly!" he gasped.

10

WIND IN THE TREES

John and Annie whirled around to look.

The shaggy brown bear was walking slowly toward the campfire. It stopped and stared at the three of them.

"Be very still," John said softly to Jack and Annie.

"Is it a grizzly?" whispered Jack.

"She is, indeed," said John. "You were right. I thought there were no grizzlies left in Yosemite. Perhaps she is the last one."

"That's sad," said Annie.

"She's beautiful, isn't she?" John said. "Can you sketch her for me?"

"Yes," whispered Annie. She reached into her pocket and took out her sketchbook.

Though he was scared of the bear, Jack did the same.

The grizzly didn't move. She stood very still and kept gazing at the three of them.

Jack's heart was pounding. By the firelight, he pressed his pencil against the white page. The pencil started moving. Soon Jack had sketched the outline of the bear. He then drew clumps of shaggy fur and big paws and claws. He darkened the bear's nose and ears.

By the time he finished his sketch, Jack wasn't afraid of the grizzly anymore. The bear *was* beautiful, just as John had said.

The grizzly huffed and shook her large head. She directed her gaze at Annie and stared at her.

"Okay, I'll tell them," Annie said to the bear.

The bear huffed again. Then she turned and lumbered back the way she had come.

"Tell us what?" John asked Annie.

"Yes, what?" said Jack, eager to hear.

"She wants us to know that she didn't mean us any harm yesterday," said Annie. "She believes all living things have a right to exist. Because she's the last grizzly bear in Yosemite, she's moving on. She's going to find a place where she's not around people, so she won't scare them anymore, a place where she can be her true self and be—"

"Wait, wait, wait, stop," said Jack.

"With other grizzly bears," finished Annie.

"She didn't say all that!" said Jack.

Annie grinned. "Trust me," she said.

John of the Mountains laughed. "I trust you, Annie," he said. "And the bear." Then he looked around. "Friends, it's nearly dark. I think you'd better return to the hotel with me."

"Oh, wow! I hear her!" said Annie, jumping up. She stared at the forest. "I hear her calling us!"

"Who? The bear?" said Jack.

"No! *Morgan!* Our teacher! She's here! I just heard her call out our names—from beyond the trees!" Annie shouted at the woods. "Hold on, Morgan! We're coming! Stay there!"

"Oh, right," said Jack. He jumped up. "Our ride home is here! Calling to us from beyond the trees!"

"I didn't hear anyone," said John.

"Really?" said Annie.

"Yes, but to be honest, I don't hear people as well as I hear nature," said John. "I will wait here by the fire awhile. If you don't soon find your teacher, promise me you will come right back."

"We will! Thank you!" said Jack. "Thank you for everything! For bringing us back here and for a great camping trip."

"We'll never forget you, John!" said Annie. "Please take our sketchbooks as a gift. And say good-bye to President Teddy for us!"

Jack and Annie handed their sketchbooks to John of the Mountains.

"Thank you, friends. I will treasure these," he said. "Have a good trip home."

"You too, John. Bye!" said Annie. Then she called toward the giant trees, "Coming, Morgan!" She grabbed Jack's hand and pulled him deeper into the forest.

"There!" said Jack. He and Annie ran to the rope ladder hanging on the other side of the giant tree.

Annie started up. Jack followed. They climbed through the dark step by step . . . step by step . . . until *finally* they reached the top of the sequoia.

By the time they slipped inside the tree house, the sky was filled with stars. The leaves of all the big trees were shaking. Far below they could barely see the glow of John's campfire.

"Good-bye, John of the Mountains. Good-bye, California," Annie said softly. "Good-bye, President Teddy and mules and last grizzly bear and—"

While Annie kept saying her good-byes, Jack started to hear a humming sound. The sound seemed to be coming from the windblown trees.

"Annie, listen," said Jack.

"Good-bye, Douglas squirrel, Alpine butterfly," said Annie, "waterfall and stars—"

"Annie, *listen!*" said Jack.

Annie stopped talking and listened to the rustling leaves of the giant trees. More and more sounds filled the evening air . . . the strange, whirring voices of all the living things of Yosemite. The wind stirred the voices together, blending them into one timeless, wordless song.

The song grew louder and louder, until it was

nearly deafening. Then suddenly it softened, died down, and stopped.

"What—what was that?" Jack said with wonder. He'd never heard anything like it.

"Nature's song," said Annie. "The song that John hears."

"Oh. Whoa," breathed Jack.

After a long moment of silence, Annie sighed. "Time to go," she said.

Jack couldn't speak.

Annie grabbed the Pennsylvania book. She found the picture of Frog Creek. "I wish we could go there!"

The wind started to blow.

The tree house started to spin.

It spun faster and faster.

Then everything was still.

Absolutely still.

The Frog Creek woods were quiet. It was early evening. No time at all had passed in Frog Creek while Jack and Annie were gone.

"We're wearing our own clothes again," said Annie. She felt in the pockets of her hoodie. "Darn. No more magic pencils."

Jack smiled. "Yeah, I loved drawing with them."

"Me too," said Annie. "Sketching nature helped me pay attention and see things better."

"Definitely," said Jack. "Maybe I'll take some art classes at the Y." He sighed. "That trip was . . ." He was at a loss for words.

"Perfect?" said Annie.

"Perfect," agreed Jack.

"We'd better go," said Annie. "We've used up half of our fourteen minutes."

"Right," said Jack. He followed Annie down the rope ladder. They stepped onto the ground and started for home.

As they walked through the evening chill, the Frog Creek woods seemed as familiar as ever.

Yet, somehow, the woods felt different, too. More mysterious and more alive, Jack thought. In the dark, he heard things he usually didn't notice: the whispering of unnamed trees, the scampering of unknown creatures, the calls of unseen birds.

"I'd like to get binoculars like Teddy's," he said, "to study birds."

"How about a magnifying glass like John's," said Annie, "to study rocks?"

"Yep, and a telescope to help learn about stars," said Jack.

"And a guide book about trees," said Annie, "and a sketchbook for drawing them."

"Definitely," said Jack. "I'd like to learn bird calls, too."

"I can teach you some," said Annie.

"Thanks. I could teach you what I know about stars," said Jack.

"Perfect," said Annie.

Jack and Annie quickened their steps and bounded out of the Frog Creek woods. High in the purple sky, the first star of the night shone above them as they ran for home.

Turn the page for a sneak peek at

Magic Tree House® Fact Tracker
Heroes for All Times

John Muir

John Muir was born in Dunbar, Scotland, in 1838. Dunbar is a cold and rainy town on the coast. John's father believed that everyone, including his children, should work hard. He was a harsh man who often beat John and his sisters and brothers.

John's grandfather taught him how to read and write. They went on long walks together along the ocean. The two spent hours exploring the seashore and its tidal

pools. John's love of nature began with his grandfather.

Wisconsin

When John was eleven, his father bought a farm in America and moved the family to Wisconsin. Instead of going to school, the Muir children had to work on the farm. Whenever he could, John explored the nearby woods and fields. He later wrote of his joy at the "young leaves, flowers, animals, the winds and the streams and the sparkling lake."

John often worked seventeen-hour days!

John's father told him that if he wanted free time, he would have to wake up early. John got up at one o'clock every morning! In these early hours, John began inventing things. He created a thermometer so sensitive that the body heat of someone standing five feet away affected it. He invented an "early-rising machine," which was an alarm clock that tipped the bed up and threw the sleeping person to the floor!

He also invented a new kind of sawmill and a horse feeder.

The machine and the drawings for it are lost, but friends of Muir described it like this.

Here's a special preview of
Magic Tree House® #36

SUNLIGHT ON THE SNOW LEOPARD

Search for the Gray Ghost of the
Mountains in Nepal with Jack and Annie!

FIRST LIGHT

A rooster crowed outside.

"Wake up, Jack! It's first light!" said Annie.

Jack opened his eyes.

Light came through the windowpanes. The fire had gone out. The room was freezing.

Jack wanted to stay in his sleeping bag. But he stretched and got up with Annie. They pulled on their parkas, hiking boots, and gloves. They rolled up their sleeping bags and pulled on their backpacks.

Annie opened the blue door, and she and Jack slipped out of Ama's Tea House.

As they hurried through the gray dawn, Jack could see his breath in the cold air. Villagers were already at work.

Small children were feeding chickens. An old woman was milking a cow. Girls were herding sheep into the frosty pasture.

Jack and Annie tramped through the tall grass. They climbed the path to Tenzin's house.

To Jack's surprise, the frail-looking man was standing outside. He wore no jacket, gloves, or shoes.

"Good morning!" Tenzin said. "Are you ready to hike up that hill?" He pointed at the rocky slope rising above his hut.

The hill looked like a high mountain to Jack! "You mean hike up that mountain?" he said.

Tenzin smiled. "Some may call it a mountain," he said. "But to me, it is only a high hill."

"What's up there?" asked Annie.

"If we are blessed, we will see the Gray Ghost," said Tenzin.

"Oh, wow," whispered Annie.

"Um . . . so the Gray Ghost isn't just a character in a story?" said Jack.

"No. She is real," said Tenzin. "Very real."

"Oh . . . she's real," Jack said in a small voice.

"You okay with that?" Annie whispered to him.

He nodded and looked back at Tenzin.

"But—don't you need warmer clothes? Or at least shoes?" Jack asked.

"I have climbed all my life without shoes," said Tenzin. "I am not afraid to do so now."

"But do you feel strong enough?" said Jack.

"Yes!" said Tenzin. "The letter you read to me last evening stirred some memories. It has brought back a bit of strength."

"So . . . how far do you think we should hike?" asked Jack.

"Until the Gray Ghost sees us," said Tenzin.

"You mean until *we* see *her*?" said Annie.

"No. She can best be seen when one is *not* looking for her," Tenzin said.

How do you not look for something that you're looking for? thought Jack.

"One can even gaze right at her and fail to see her," said Tenzin.

"So, what does one do to find her?" Annie asked.

"One can only hope to be in the right place at the right time," said Tenzin.

Annie smiled. "I understand," she said.

She does? thought Jack.

"Good. Then let us begin our journey!" said Tenzin. He turned and started hiking up the rock-covered slope behind his hut.

"Ready?" Annie asked Jack.

"No. Listen—we shouldn't encourage him," said Jack. "Ama said he's not been well. He's not dressed warmly enough, and he's not making sense. We have to stop him."

"How?" said Annie.

"I don't know," said Jack. Then he shouted, "TENZIN!"

Tenzin turned around and waved at them.

"Leave your backpacks by my door!" he shouted. "Follow me to higher ground!" And he started hiking up the slope again.

"Oh, man," said Jack. "What should we do?"

"Wait, wait—did he just say *higher ground*?" said Annie. She grabbed Morgan's note from her pocket. She read aloud:

Ask those around you
Where the ghost can be found.
Follow the one
Who says "higher ground."

"Yes! Tenzin said Morgan's words!" said Annie. "He *literally* said, *Follow me to higher ground!*"

"Whoa," said Jack.

"So we *have* to follow him!" said Annie. "We don't have a choice!"

Jack took a deep breath. "You're right," he said.

He and Annie set their backpacks outside Tenzin's door. Then they started up the rocky slope, following Tenzin to higher ground.